THE EDUCATION OF

The Education of the Stoic

THE ONLY MANUSCRIPT OF THE BARON OF TEIVE

BY FERNANDO PESSOA

EDITED & TRANSLATED BY RICHARD ZENITH
PREFACE BY FRANÇOISE LAYE
AFTERWORDS BY
ANTONIO TABUCCHI & RICHARD ZENITH

EXACT CHANGE ❧ CAMBRIDGE ❧ 2005

Cover photographs by Naomi Yang

Exact Change books are edited by Damon Krukowski
and designed by Naomi Yang

Exact Change
5 Brewster Street, Cambridge, MA 02138
www.exactchange.com

Distributed by D.A.P. / Distributed Art Publishers
155 Sixth Avenue, 2nd floor, New York, NY 10013
www.artbook.com

Printed on acid-free recycled paper

❖❖❖ CONTENTS ❖❖❖

ABOUT THE BARON OF TEIVE

FRANÇOISE LAYE

IT IS IMPOSSIBLE TO PUBLISH THE BARON OF TEIVE without remembering Bernardo Soares. Both "heteronyms" were connected to *The Book of Disquiet* — Soares as its ultimate author, and Teive as a quasi-author* — and Pessoa created them as parallel personalities, or rather, as face-to-face opposites, mirror reflections of each other. The Baron of Teive / Bernardo Soares; *The Education of the Stoic / The Book of Disquiet*. The antithesis is radical and yet, as Richard Zenith explains in his "postmortem," the two terms are intimately linked.

The Baron of Teive is assigned a tragic and fascinating destiny: a search for perfection reminiscent of Mallarmé's quest but pursued, with relentless logic, to the bitter end. It is this implacable quality in the baron that contrasts so sharply with the endless evasions, self-analysis and introspection of Bernardo Soares. *The Book of Disquiet* is the book of despair, *The Education of the Stoic* the book of suicide — not only of a man but of a creator coming up against his own limits.

---

* Though Pessoa never directly named the Baron of Teive as a possible "author" of *The Book of Disquiet*, he left half a dozen passages signed by the baron in a large envelope with material for *The Book*, whose fictional authorship shifted over the years. It's likely that Pessoa considered making Teive at least a collaborating author. [–ED.]

Pessoa fashioned this psychological portrait with rare mastery, even at the stylistic level. If one of the constants of *The Book of Disquiet* is its prolixity, with multiply overlapping planes of reflection and with all the meanders of a thinking mind trying desperately to get at the mystery of existence, the prose of the Baron of Teive admits of no detours, no narcissistic digressions. With its perfectly rectilinear movement, it heads straight toward its goal, like an arrow — and each hit is fatal. There is, indeed, something ruthless in the style, as there is in the person of the baron, whose final meeting with himself is his meeting with death. And the reader is the fascinated witness of this drama of dissection, played out with surgical precision to its foregone conclusion.

RICHARD ZENITH

IN *THE EDUCATION OF THE STOIC* THE BARON of Teive proposes "to offer a simple explanation" of why he wasn't able to produce finished literary works, but even that explanation was left as a bunch of inconclusive, unconnected fragments. As in a set of Chinese boxes, *The Education* is one of many works — within the chaos of Pessoa's lifework — that remained vastly unfinished, hopelessly unstructured, and practically unknown. Pessoa published none of Teive's writings and mentioned him in only one of his numerous self-interpretive texts (cited in the "postmortem"). Despite the dearth of explicit references, Pessoa wrote abundantly and earnestly in the baron's name, probably one of the heteronyms "yet to appear" mentioned in his letter of 28 July 1932 to João Gaspar Simões, his future biographer.

Teive's public "appearance" did not occur until twenty-eight years later, in 1960, when the scholar Maria Aliete Galhoz published several prose passages signed by the aristocratic heteronym. Teresa Rita Lopes published additional passages in 1990, but the baron remained a shadowy, enigmatic figure until 1999, the year of the first Portuguese edition of *A Educação do Estóico*, which gathered together all the writings of Teive found in Pessoa's notoriously labyrinthine archives, which are housed at the National Library in Lisbon. Many of those writings were typed or handwritten on loose sheets, but I found the oldest and most revealing nucleus of Teive's work in a small black notebook whose contents had never been transcribed. Difficult to decipher and following no logical sequence, the material from the notebook consists largely of notes and sketches that the author intended to flesh out and rework later on. He did rework some of the material into finished, typewritten pieces, but most of it was left like the rest of Teive's work — as "sudden, ingenious ideas... but disconnected, in need of articulation" — which the baron says he burned up in his fireplace.

If the material from the black notebook were presented in a separate section, without altering the order of its now longer, now shorter, but consistently discontinuous fragments, readers would be able to follow the author's creative drive as it shifts from idea to idea, from topic to topic, now backtracking, now rushing ahead, now jumping to a different track. Unfortunately many of the fragments, left stranded and without a context, would become lost in this chaotic stream, or the reader would get lost. And so I chose to weave into a single narrative the material from the notebook and the passages written or typed on loose sheets, joining up certain "biographical" details that were textually detached (two short fragments about Teive's childhood, for instance), or uniting scattered reflections on a common theme. This doesn't mean surgery, for the integrity of each autonomous passage has been respected, nor is this a factitious reconstruction of a body that never existed. It's merely an attempt to better display the stones — whether chiseled and smoothed or still in the rough — of a monument that never got off the ground.

Pessoa's original title for this work was *The Only Manuscript of the Baron of Teive*, recorded in the black notebook (where Pessoa initially wrote "Last Manuscript," changing it immediately to "Only"). This became a subtitle (along with "the impossibility of producing superior art") on the loose sheet that gives *The Education of the Stoic* as the title, which may or may not have been Pessoa's ultimate preference, assuming he had a definite preference. Yet another title, *The Profession of Nonproducer*, appears at the top of one of the typed passages.

The Appendix contains five thematically relevant prose pieces. If "The Duel" may have been written long before the Baron of Teive existed, "Three Pessimists" and "Leopardi" — both written in English — seem to date from the same period as the nobleman (1928 on). Certain sentences read like translations of Teive's prose into English, and the English is rather contaminated by Portuguese syntax, a phenomenon that intensified as the years separating Pessoa from his South African childhood increased. (Pessoa lived in the English colony of Natal from age seven to seventeen, and he wrote much of his subsequent prose and poetry in English.) The fourth piece, "In the Garden of Epictetus," is relevant in a negative sense, for it represents what, in his "education," the baron *didn't* learn from the renowned Stoic philosopher. The final piece, published by Pessoa in a newspaper in 1934, takes Coleridge's explanation of how he wrote "Kubla Khan" as a metaphor for the inevitably fragmentary nature of all literary creation. By indicting human weakness generally as an impediment to making complete works of art, Pessoa implicitly justifies the baron's (and his own) failure to produce any (or many) finished literary works, since they were, after all, only human.

This translation is of the complete text as published in the second Portuguese edition, where detailed information is provided on the archive sources and the ordering of the passages. The notes in this edition elucidate literary and historical references and list only the more significant alternate words and phrases found in the margins of the manuscripts. Six-dot ellipses in brackets [......] are used to indicate unfinished sentences and blank space left by the author for one or more words within a sentence; illegible words or phrases are indicated by a three-dot ellipsis in brackets [...].

Of those people whose help I acknowledged in the Portuguese edition, I feel I should rename Manuela Parreira da Silva, who greatly assisted me in the arduous task of deciphering the pages in the black notebook signed by the Baron of Teive. This English-language edition, in the shape it has taken, was enabled by Alexandra Lucas Coelho, Amy Hundley, Antonio Tabucchi, Françoise Laye, Martin Earl and Morgan Entrekin. My thanks to all.

The Education of the Stoic

The Only Manuscript of the Baron of Teive

The Impossibility of Producing Superior Art

Manuscript found in a drawer [1]

Rather than leave my book on top of the desk, where it might be picked up by some hotel worker's not very clean hands, I decided to put it in the drawer, which I almost had to force open. Pushing the book into the drawer, I felt it hit against something, for I knew that the drawer couldn't be that short.

We've been devastated by the severest and deadliest drought in history — that of our profound awareness of the futility of all effort and the vanity of all plans.

✳

I've reached the height of emptiness, the plenitude of nothing at all. What will lead me to commit suicide is the same kind of urge that makes one go to bed early. I'm tired to death of all intentions.

Nothing at this point can change my life.

If... If...

Yes, but if is always something that never happened, and if it never happened, why imagine what it would be if it had?

✳

I sense that the end of my life is near, because I want it to be near. I spent the last two days burning, one by one (and it took two days because I sometimes reread them), all of my manuscripts, the notes of my deceased thoughts, the sketches and even some finished passages of the works

I would never have written. It was without hesitation, but with a lingering grief, that I made this sacrifice by which I take my leave — like a man who burns a bridge — from the shore of this life I'm about to abandon. I'm freed. I'm ready. I'm going to kill myself. But I'd at least like to leave an intellectual memoir of my life, a written picture — as accurate as I can make it — of what I was on the inside. Since I wasn't able to leave a succession of beautiful lies, I want to leave the smidgen of truth that the falsehood of everything lets us suppose we can tell.

This will be my only manuscript. I leave it not, as Bacon, to the charitable thoughts of future generations,[2] but (without comparison) to the consideration of those whom the future will make my peers.

Having broken all ties but the last between me and life, I've acquired an emotional clarity in my soul and a mental clarity in my intellect that give me the force of words, not to achieve the literary work I could never have achieved, but to offer at least a simple explanation of why I didn't achieve it.

These pages are not my confession; they're my definition. And I feel, as I begin to write it, that I can write with some semblance of truth.

The suicide victim was too hasty in his judgment. In fact the newspaper reports paid him all due homage. The local correspondent for the Diário de Notícias,[3] for instance, conveyed the news of his death in these words:

> Senhor Álvaro Coelho de Athayde, the 20th Baron of Teive, committed suicide yesterday, at his estate in Macieira. He was from one of the most prominent families in the district. The sad end of the Baron of Teive caused considerable dismay, as he was admired by one and all for his unimpeachable character.
>
> The Macieira Estate
> July 12, 1920

There's no greater tragedy than an equal intensity, in the same soul or the same man, of the intellectual sentiment and the moral sentiment. For a man to be utterly and absolutely moral, he has to be a bit stupid. For a man to be absolutely intellectual, he has to be a bit immoral. I don't know what game or irony of creation makes it impossible for man to be both things at once. And yet, to my misfortune, this duality occurs in me. Endowed with both virtues, I've never been able to make myself into anything. It wasn't a surfeit of one quality, but of two, that made me unfit to live life.

Whenever and wherever I had an actual or potential rival, I promptly gave up, without a moment's hesitation. It's one of the few things in life about which I never hesitated. My pride could never stand the idea of me competing with someone else, particularly since it would mean the horrid possibility of defeat. I refused, for the same reason, to take part in competitive games. If I lost, I always fumed with resentment. Because I thought I was better than everyone else? No: I never thought I was better in chess or in whist. It was because of sheer pride, a ruthless and raging pride that my mind's most desperate efforts could do nothing to curb or stanch. I kept my distance from life and the world, and an encounter with any of their elements always offended me like an insult from below, like the sudden defiance of a universal lackey.

In times of painful doubt, when I knew from the start that I'd go wrong, what made me furious at myself was the disproportionate weight of the social factor in my decisions. I was never able to overcome the influence of heredity and my upbringing. I could pooh-pooh the sterile concepts of nobility and social rank, but I never succeeded in forgetting them. They're like an inborn cowardice, which I loathe and struggle against but which binds my mind and my will with inscrutable ties. Once I had the chance to marry a simple girl who could perhaps have made me happy, but between me and her, in my soul's indecision, stood fourteen generations of barons, a mental image of the whole town smirking at my wedding, the sarcasm of friends I'm not even close to, and a huge uneasiness made of mean and petty thoughts — so many petty thoughts that it weighed on me like the commission of a crime. And so I, the man of reason and detachment, lost out on happiness because of the neighbors I disdain.

How I'd dress, how I'd act, how I'd receive people in my house (where perhaps I wouldn't have to receive anyone), all the uncouth expressions and naïve attitudes that her affection wouldn't veil nor her devotion make me forget — all of this loomed like a specter of serious things, as if it were an argument, on sleepless nights when I tried to defend my desire to have her in the endless web of impossibilities that has always entangled me.

I still remember — so vividly I can smell the gentle fragrance of the spring air — the afternoon when I decided, after thinking everything over, to abdicate from love as from an insoluble problem. It was in May, a May that was softly summery, with the flowers around my estate already in full bloom, their colors fading as the sun made its slow descent. Escorted by regrets and self-reproach, I walked among my few trees. I had dined early and was wandering, alone like a symbol, under the useless shadows and faint rustle of leaves. And suddenly I was overwhelmed by a desire to renounce completely, to withdraw once and for all, and I felt an intense nausea for having had so many desires, so many hopes, with so many outer conditions for attaining them and so much inner impossibility of really wanting to attain them. That soft and sad moment marks the beginning of my suicide.

＊

...the weak, involuntary asceticism of those in whom the intelligence is like the circulation of blood — an essential condition for life, one of life's organic foundations.

The air gently wafted on that autumn evening, and the distant mountains stood out with cold clarity against the sky, but I didn't think about them much. I focused only on my thoughts; everything I had lived seemed sadder to me than if it had never been.

∗

(my childhood)

...the gratification of all my whims and desires, which in fact amounted to little more than my wish to be alone.

∗

Resentful and vindictive as a child, in my teenage years I lost that mean-spiritedness that comes from being oversensitive. (I suppose that the development in me of the capacity for abstract thought had something to do with this.) But I've retained, in a modified form, the essence of what I was. I still get rankled when I lose an idea, or forget a phrase I wanted to write down, or fail to remember a particular point of view. I realize that I would frequently be unable to give physical shape to these rough outlines. But I'm jealous of my own self, I'm greedy for the abstract, and I've noticed that greed and vindictiveness, perhaps because they're both forms of mean-spiritedness, are of the same flesh and blood.

∗

Sudden, ingenious ideas that were partly expressed in exactly the right words and that could have been raised into monuments — but disconnected, in need of articulation... And my will wouldn't collaborate if it had to have aesthetics as a partner and couldn't leave the thoughts in isolated paragraphs of a potential story — just a bunch of sentences that sounded striking but that would only really have been striking if I'd written the story in which they were expressive moments, pithy observations, linking phrases... Some were witty sayings, ingenious but unintelligible without the surrounding text that was never written.

*

I'm going to end a life that I thought could contain every kind of greatness but that in fact consisted only of my incapacity to really want to be great. Whenever I arrived at a certainty, I remembered that those with the greatest certainties are lunatics.

Attention to detail and a perfectionist instinct, far from stimulating action, are character qualities that lead to renunciation. Better to dream than to be. It's so easy to achieve what we want in dreams!

A thousand ideas in a jumble, each one a poem, flourishing without rhyme or reason. They were so numerous that I can't remember when they came to me, much less when I lost them.

Small emotions are what remain. A breeze on a still stretch of countryside can roil my soul. A distant blast of music from the village band evokes an array of sounds in me more complex than those of a symphony orchestra. An old lady on a doorstep makes my heart melt. A dirty child in my path illuminates me. A sparrow perched on a wire delights me in a way I can't explain, like a vision inextricably tied to truth itself.

✳

I belong to a generation — assuming that this generation includes others besides me — that lost its faith in the gods of the old religions as well as in the gods of modern nonreligions. I reject Jehovah as I reject humanity. For me, Christ and progress are both myths from the same world. I don't believe in the Virgin Mary, and I don't believe in electricity.

I was always millimetric in my thinking, meticulous both in the language of my writing and in the organization of the ideas I wanted to express.

My mother's death broke the last of the outer ties that still made me feel attached to life. At first I felt dizzy —

not with the kind of dizziness that makes the body reel but the kind that's like a dead emptiness in the brain, an instinctive awareness of the void. And the tedium that until then I had experienced as anxiety wilted into sheer boredom.

Her love, which I'd never especially felt when she was alive, became all too clear to me once I'd lost her.

I discovered, through its absence (which is how we discover the true worth of anything), that I needed affection — that it's something we breathe, like air, without feeling it.

I have all the conditions for happiness, save happiness. The conditions are detached from one another.

I'm the maturity of what Chateaubriand's René[4] was the adolescence. The outer form is different, but our substance is identical — the same mental self-absorption, the same dissatisfaction.

Underneath all their anxieties, adolescents still have the blind will to live. Rousseau [......], but he commanded Europe. Chateaubriand whined and daydreamed, but he was a state minister. Vigny[5] saw his plays put on stage. Antero de Quental[6] preached socialism. Leopardi was a philologist.[7]

I lay down my pen without laying it down and see, through my window that looks out onto the dark countryside, the light of the high and round moon permeating the air like a new, visible air. How often a sight like this has accompanied me during my endless meditations, useless dreams, sleepless nights when I can't work or write.

My heart feels like an inorganic weight.

In the perfectly black silence of stock-still dawns, their profile stands out as if truth existed.

*

It is impossible to live life according to reason. Intelligence provides no guiding rule. This realization unveiled for me what is perhaps hidden in the myth of the Fall. As when one's physical gaze is struck by lightning, my soul's vision was struck by the terrible and true meaning of the temptation that led Adam to eat from the so-called Tree of Knowledge.

Where intelligence exists, life is impossible.

*

My radical renunciation of all metaphysical speculation and my moral disgust at all attempts to systematize the unknown do not derive, as in most of those who share this attitude, from an inability to speculate. I've thought long and hard, and I know.

I began by elaborating a kind of psychological epistemology. To help me understand systems, I created a method for analyzing those who produce them. I don't claim to have discovered that a philosophy is no more than the expression of a temperament. Others, I suppose, have already discovered this. But I discovered, for my own orientation, that a temperament is a philosophy.

Self-preoccupation, in literary or philosophical matters, has always struck me as a lack of good manners. People who write forget that they're speaking in written form, and many write things they would never dare say. There are some who fill up page after page with explanations and analyses of their own self, and yet they would never — or many of them would never — presume to weary an audience, no matter how receptive, with a recital of their personalities.

Pessimism, I have noticed, is quite often a result of sexual rejection. This is clearly the case in Leopardi and Antero de Quental. I can only see a system built on one's sexual problems as a hopelessly vile and crude thing. All crude individuals need the sexual leitmotif; it's what distinguishes them, in fact. They can't tell jokes that aren't sexual; they can't be witty without referring to sex. They see in all couples a sexual reason for their being couples.

What does the universe have to do with someone's sexual problems?

I realize that in this manuscript I violate the principle I've laid down. But these pages are a testament, and in testaments the testator can't avoid talking about himself. There's more tolerance for the dying, and these words come from a dying man.[8]

✳

Our problem isn't that we're individualists. It's that our individualism is static rather than dynamic. We value what we think rather than what we do. We forget that we haven't done, or been, what we thought; that the first function of life is action, just as the first property of things is motion.

Giving importance to what we think because we thought it, taking our own selves not only (to quote the Greek philosopher)[9] as the measure of all things but as their norm or standard, we create in ourselves, if not an interpretation, at least a criticism of the universe, which we don't even know and therefore cannot criticize. The giddiest, most weak-minded of us then promote that criticism to an interpretation — an interpretation that's superimposed, like a hallucination; induced rather than deduced. It's a hallucination in the strict sense, being an illusion based on something only dimly seen.

Modern man, if he's unhappy, is a pessimist.

There's something contemptible, something degrading, in this projection of our personal sorrows onto the whole universe. There's something shamefully egocentric in supposing that the universe is inside us, or that we're a kind of nucleus and epitome, or symbol, of it.

The fact that I suffer may be an impediment to the existence of an unequivocally good Creator, but it doesn't prove the nonexistence of a Creator, or the existence of an evil Creator, or even the existence of a neutral Creator. It proves only that evil exists in the world — something which can hardly be called a discovery, and which no one has yet tried to deny.

Consciously or unconsciously, we give importance to our feelings just because they're ours, and we often call this inner vanity pride, just as we call all sorts of truths our truth.

It was Antero de Quental more than any other poet who gave expression to the conflict that ravages our soul, for he possessed feeling and intelligence with equal intensity. I refer to the conflict between the emotional need for faith and the intellectual impossibility of believing.

I've finally arrived at these brief precepts for an intellectual rule of life.

I don't regret having burned all the sketches for my literary works. That's all I had to bequeath to the world.

Whatever may be the secret of the world's mystery, it must be either very complex or else very simple, but of a simplicity that can't be humanly grasped. My complaint against the majority of philosophical theories is that they're simplistic, and the proof is in the fact that they attempt to explain, since to explain is to simplify.

However fanciful Soame Jenyns's theory of evil[10] may be, at least it's not absurd, like the notion of a good and all-powerful god who created evil, since he created everything. Soame Jenyns's hypothesis at least has the clear, though perhaps illusory, advantage of analogy. In the same way that we intervene — sometimes for their good, sometimes for evil; perhaps sometimes for their good when we meant to do evil, and vice-versa — in the lives of beings inferior to us, it's possible that our lives are subject to intervention from beings as superior to us as we are to the cattle of our fields and the birds of our sky.

It once occurred to me — more out of idle speculation than real belief — that since life is the law of all existence, death must always result from an outside intervention, meaning that every death is a violent one. Some deaths are visibly violent, and we ourselves cause many of those; other, so-called natural deaths might be equally violent but caused by beings imperceptible to our senses. Just as nations, no matter how decadent, only terminate through invasions and violence from outside, so

it might be with the end of human lives. Suicide itself —
it occurred to me during my logical reverie — could be
a compulsion from outside; no life would spontaneously
end itself, but in suicide the instrument of death would
be the selfsame victim. I would have forgotten all about
this frivolous speculation had it not once saved me from
committing suicide — a long time ago, shortly after grad-
uating from university. My life was wracked by anguish,
but the vague possibility that my theory could be right
(for it had as much chance of being right as any other)
and my unwillingness — if it was right — to perform a
servile act as someone else's instrument prevented me (I
don't know if for better or worse) from taking the step
that, as it turns out, was merely postponed until now.

*

I've never been able to believe that I, or that anyone, could
offer any effective relief for human ills, much less cure
them. But I've never been able to ignore them either.
The tiniest human anguish — even the slightest thought
of one — has always upset and anguished me, prevent-
ing me from focusing just on myself. My conviction that
all remedies for the soul are useless should naturally lift
me to a summit of indifference, below which the clouds
of that same conviction would cover from view all the
hubbub on earth. But powerful as thought is, it can do
nothing to quell rebellious emotions. We can't choose
not to feel, as we can not to walk. And so I witness, as

I've always witnessed, ever since I can remember feeling with the higher emotions, all the pain, injustice and misery that's in the world, as a paralytic might witness the drowning of a man whom no one, however able-bodied, could save. In me the pain of others became more than a simple pain: there was the pain of seeing it, the pain of seeing that it was incurable, and the pain of knowing that my awareness of its incurableness precluded even the useless noble-mindedness of wishing I felt like doing something to cure it. My lack of initiative was the root cause of all my troubles — of my inability to want something before having thought about it, of my inability to commit myself, of my inability to decide in the only way one can decide: by deciding, not by thinking. I'm like Buridan's donkey,[11] dying at the mathematical midpoint between the water of emotion and the hay of action; if I didn't think, I might still die, but it wouldn't be from thirst or hunger.

Whatever I think or feel inevitably turns into a form of inertia. Thought, which for other people is a compass to guide action, is for me its microscope, making me see whole universes to span where a footstep would have sufficed, as if Zeno's argument about the impossibility of crossing a given space — which, being infinitely divisible, is therefore infinite — were a strange drug that had intoxicated my psychological self. And feeling, which in other people enters the will like a hand in a glove, or like a fist in the guard of a sword, was always in me another form of thought — futile like a rage that makes us tremble so much we can't move, or like a panic (the panic, in my case, of feeling too intensely) that freezes the frightened man in his tracks,[12] when his fright should make him flee.

My whole life has been a battle lost on the map. Cowardice didn't even make it to the battlefield, where perhaps it would have dissipated; it haunted the chief of staff in his office, all alone with his certainty of defeat. He didn't dare implement his battle plan, since it was sure to be imperfect, and he didn't dare perfect it (though it could never be truly perfect), since his conviction that it would never be perfect killed all his desire to strive for perfection. Nor did it ever occur to him that his plan, though imperfect, might be closer to perfection than the enemy's. The truth is that my real enemy, victorious over me since God, was that very idea of perfection, marching against me at the head of all the troops of the world — in the tragic vanguard of all the world's armed men.[13]

*

The abstract always impressed me more deeply than the concrete. I remember as a child not being afraid of anybody, nor even of animals, but I was scared of dark rooms... I remember how that apparent oddity disrupted the otherwise simple psychology that enveloped me.

I was also, contrary to what's normal, more afraid of death than of dying. I even scorned, and still scorn, suffering. I've always valued my consciousness over all the agreeable sensations of my body. The only time I was operated on (recently, when my left leg was amputated), I refused to be put to sleep. I agreed only to a local anesthetic.[14]

If today I take the path of self-inflicted death, it's because I can no longer tolerate the [...] of the condemned man. It's not moral suffering that leads me to commit suicide but the moral vacuum responsible for that suffering.

My present state of mind is of the sort that gives rise to great mysticisms and transcendental renunciations; they, however, are founded on faith, and I have no faith. In fact it's my not having faith, either because I'm unable or don't know how to have it, that's at the origin of this vacuum that's my consciousness of the world.

...when I dueled, in Paris, with the Marquis of Plombières.

I naturally consider duels to be ridiculous. But since, like everyone else, I've always actively or passively accepted social conventions and enjoyed their advantages (beginning with the social prestige of my title), I felt it would have been unseemly to evade one of those conventions just because it was the only one that placed me in danger.

The realization that I was far more likely to be wounded than killed immediately inhibited me from commenting on the matter. I never feared suffering; I not only scorned it, I scorned any and all preoccupation with suffering. It was attitudes like this one that thwarted my ambition to comment in the abstract.

It's curious how my greatest worry in the duel — the one that eclipsed all others — was that I would be "bested" by my adversary, that I would prove to be his inferior on the field. I've always recognized, as a deplorable but indomitable characteristic, that I can't stand to lose, and my fear that I'd be unable to conceal my resentment always made me shy away from games and competitions — from any activity that would pit me against someone else. This, I confess, would almost have induced me to get out of the duel, could I have done so gracefully.

✳

(The seduction of Maria Adelaide)[15]

They (the licentious) discover unexplored sides of human feelings; they shed light on sensitive things shrouded in darkness, despite the carnal contact that occurs.

✳

Why the Baron didn't seduce more girls.[16]

I did eventually seduce a few, and I looked ridiculous in my own eyes, without excuse [......]

✳

I could easily have seduced any of the housemaids in my service. But some were too big, or seemed big because they were so vivacious, and in their presence I felt automatically shy, unnerved; I couldn't even dream of seducing them. Others were too small, or delicate, and I felt sorry for them. Others were unattractive. And so I passed by the specific phenomenon of love as I passed, more or less, by the general phenomenon of life.

The fear of hurting others, the sensuality aroused by physical acts, my awareness of the real existence of other souls — these things were trammels to my life, and I ask myself now what good they did me, or anybody else. The girls I didn't seduce were seduced by others, for it was inevitable that somebody seduce them. I had scruples where other men didn't think twice, and after seeing what I didn't do done by others, I wondered: Why did I think so much if it only made me suffer?

✳

Scruples are the death of action. Whoever thinks about other people's feelings is certain not to act. There is no action, no matter how small (and the greater the action, the truer this statement), that doesn't wound another soul, that doesn't hurt someone, that doesn't have aspects we can't help but regret, if we have a heart. I've often thought that the hermit's true philosophy isn't based on the notion of seclusion for its own sake but on the rejection of the hostile behavior that results from the simple fact of living.

*

I saw other people do the things I'd avoided because I felt they were banal, and when I saw what they'd done, I realized they were the most normal things in the world.

*

The subconscious secret of the ordinary man: to live the romantic side of things energetically and life's coarser side romantically.

Teach nothing, for you still have everything to learn.

A dream, when too lifelike or familiar, becomes a new reality, equally tyrannical; it ceases to be a refuge. Dreamed armies ultimately go down in defeat, just like those that go under in the battles and clashes of the world.

✳

Dreaming, daydreaming — that wispiness of spirit like in those who sigh at fashion plates, princes and princesses, the beloved, celebrities — is a tendency I've always considered vile and loathsome.

✳

I rejected dreaming as a madman's or schoolgirl's vice. But I also rejected reality or, rather, it rejected me; I'm not sure whether due to my incompetence, my despondency, or my failure to understand it. Neither form of enjoyment was possible for me — neither the kiss of reality, nor the caress of the imaginary.[17]

I have no complaints about those who surround me or once surrounded me. No one ever treated me badly in any way. Everybody treated me well, but with detachment. I soon realized that the detachment was in me, that it came from me. That's why I can say, with no illusions, that I've always been respected. I've never been loved. Today I realize that I couldn't have been. I had admirable qualities and strong emotions [......], but I didn't have what's known as love.

...people of my spiritual race — Rousseau, Chateaubriand, Senancour, Amiel.[18] But Rousseau stirred up the world, Chateaubriand [......], Amiel at least left a diary. I'm a more extreme example of the disease that we all suffered, because I didn't leave anything at all.

✳

I've never felt nostalgia, because I've never had anything to feel nostalgic about, and my mind has always ruled my feelings. Having never done anything with my life, I have nothing to wistfully remember. I once had hopes — since what doesn't exist can be anything — but I no longer hope, for I don't see why the future should be different from the past. Some people miss the past just because it *is* the past, and even what was bad seems good to them, for the simple reason that it's gone forever, along with who they were when it happened. The mere abstraction of time never meant enough to me that I could pine after my past just because it's long gone, or because I was younger then than I am now. Besides, to pine after the past for these reasons is something that anybody can do, and I refuse to be like just anybody.

I've never felt nostalgia. There's no period of my life I remember without chagrin. In all of them I was the same: the one who lost the game or didn't deserve whatever paltry victory he won.

Yes, I had hopes, because not to hope is to die.

The struggle is ever more difficult, my hope ever more sluggish, and the disparity between what I am and what I thought I could be forever more pronounced in the night of my relentless futility.

∗

I first realized how utterly disinterested I was in myself and in what I once held closest to heart when one day, going home, I heard a fire alarm that seemed to be in my neighborhood. It occurred to me that my house might be in flames (though it wasn't, after all), and whereas I once would have been possessed by horror at the thought of all my manuscripts going up in smoke, I noticed, to my astonishment, that the possibility of my house being on fire left me indifferent, almost glad in the thought of how much simpler my life would be without those manuscripts. In the past, the loss of my manuscripts — of my life's fragmentary but carefully wrought oeuvre — would have driven me mad, but now I viewed the prospect as a casual incident of my fate, not as a fatal blow that would annihilate my personality by annihilating its manifestations.

I began to understand how the continuous struggle for an unattainable perfection finally tires us out, and I understood the great mystics and great ascetics, who recognize life's futility in their soul. What of me would be lost in those written sheets? Before, I would have said "everything." Today I'd say "nothing," or "not much," or "something strange."

I had become, to myself, an objective reality. But in doing so I couldn't tell if I had found myself or lost myself.

✳

Could it be my house that's on fire? Could it be that all my manuscripts, the entire expression of my entire life, will go up in flames? The mere idea of such a catastrophe used to make me tremble with horror. And then one day I suddenly realized — I no longer know whether with or without horror, whether with or without astonishment — that I wouldn't care if they went up in flames. What secret wellspring that was mine alone had dried up in my soul?

I realized then that year after aridly weary year had filled the depths of my soul with an equally arid and profound weariness. I had fallen asleep, and all my soul's privileges — its desires that dream exaltedly, its emotions that dream intensely, and its anxieties that dream inversely — had fallen asleep with me.

✳

...something I'm unable to define except as a physical aversion to life.

To think like spiritualists and act like materialists. It's not an absurd creed; it's the spontaneous creed of all humanity.

What's the life of humanity but a religious evolution with no influence on daily life?

Humanity is attracted to what's ideal, and the loftier and less human the ideal, the more attractive it will be to the praxis (if it's progressive) of humanity's civilized life, which thus passes from nation to nation, from era to era, from civilization to civilization. Civilized humanity opens its arms to a religion that preaches chastity, to a religion that preaches equality, to a religion that preaches peace. But normal humanity procreates, discriminates, and clashes continuously, and will do so for as long as it lasts.

*

At the same time and in the same society, the normal man who's an atheist conducts his life in the same way as the normal man who's a theist, even though it would seem that they should act alike in few things. There's no thesis or theory that affects the atmosphere we breathe. Astrology is a world apart, like dreams. Astrology, if we choose to believe in it, is just a name we give to a form from the realm of the imagination. A novel and a treatise on astrology are novels with different themes, differing less from each other than a cloak-and-dagger novel from a social novel, or a detective story from a love story.[19]

But when I read Rousseau or Chateaubriand or [......], I realize with horror that my veneration of what's objective, of what's real [......], doesn't exempt me from an appalling, visceral identity with them. Pages by certain of them trouble me; they seem to have been written not by me but — through an absurdity curiously appropriate to me — by a twin brother I never had, someone who is differently the same as me.

I don't, after all, admire the Greeks. They always gave me the impression, I won't say of outright falseness, but of inordinate simplicity. Compared to us they're children, with the charm but also the incompleteness of children. Even their superior qualities are those in which children — conserving what's different [...] — have the advantage over adults. Growing up, they gained in complexity, which was not entirely to their advantage, for they lost that childish spontaneity in emotion and sensation, which nobody had like the Greeks; they lost the child's clear and implacable way of reasoning, which the Greeks had like nobody else; they lost that simple and direct egoism, that fresh and so human imagination, and that careful elaboration of facts — all of which distinguished the Greeks in life, in thought, and in art. Certain contributions of the Greeks even seem like children's games they made up, such as elections by drawing straws, or the democratic participation of an army's soldiers — on an equal footing with their commanders — in decisions about the very campaigns they waged.

✳

To think that I considered this incoherent heap of half-written scraps a literary work! To think, in this decisive moment, that I believed myself capable of organizing all these pieces into a finished, visible whole! If the organizational power of thought were enough to make the work materialize, if this organization could be achieved by the emotional intensity that suffices for a short poem or brief essay, then the work I aspired to would have doubtless taken shape, for it would have shaped itself in me, without my help as a determining agent.

Had I concentrated on what was possible for my unaggressive will, I know I could have produced short essays from the fragments of my unachievable masterpiece. I could have put together several miscellanies of finished, well-rounded prose pieces. I could have collected many of the phrases scattered among my notes into more than just a book of thoughts, and it wouldn't be superficial or banal.

My pride, however, won't let me settle for less than my mind is capable of. I've never allowed myself to go halfway, to accept anything less in the work I do than my whole personality and entire ambition. Had I felt that my mind was incapable of synthetic work, I would have bridled my pride, seeing it as a form of madness. But the deficiency wasn't in my mind, which was always very good at synthesizing and organizing. The problem was in my lukewarm will to make the enormous effort that a finished whole requires.

By this standard perhaps no creative work anywhere would ever have been made. I realize that. I realize that if all the great minds had scrupulously desired to do only what was perfect, or at least (since perfection is impossible) what was in complete accord with their entire personality, then they would have given up, like me.

Only those who are more willful than intelligent, more impulsive than rational, have a part to play in the real life of this world. *Disjecta membra*, said Carlyle,[20] is what remains of any poet, or of any man. But an intense pride, like the one that killed me and will yet kill me, won't admit the idea of subjecting to the humiliation of future ages the deformed, mutilated body that inhabits and defines the soul whose inevitable imperfection it expresses.

Where the soul's dignity is concerned, I can see no middle course or intermediate term between the ascetic and the common man. If you're a doer, then do; if a renouncer, then renounce. Do with the brutality that doing entails; renounce with the absoluteness of renunciation. Renounce without tears or self-pity, noble at least in the vehemence of your renunciation. Disdain yourself, but with dignity.

To weep before the world — and the more beautiful the weeping, the more the world opens up to the weeper, and the more public is his shame — this is the ultimate indignity that can be wreaked on the inner life by a defeated man who didn't keep his sword to do his final duty as a soldier. We are all soldiers in this instinctive regiment called life; we must live by the law of reason or by no law. Gaiety is for dogs; whining is for women. Man has only his honor and silence. I felt this more than ever while watching the flames in the fireplace consume my writings once and for all.

There's something vile — and all the more vile because ridiculous — in the tendency of feeble men to make universal tragedies out of the sad comedies of their private woes.

My recognition of this fact has always prevented me — unjustly, I realize — from experiencing the full emotion of the great pessimistic poets. My disenchantment only increased when I read about their lives. The three great pessimistic poets of the last century — Leopardi, Vigny and Antero de Quental — became unbearable to me. The sexual basis of their pessimism, after I'd discerned it in their works and confirmed it in their life stories, left a nauseous feeling in my mind. I realize what a tragedy it can be for any man — and especially for a sensitive man like any of the three named poets —

to be deprived, for whatever reason, of sexual relations, as occurred with Leopardi and Quental, or to not have relations of the kind and frequency desired, as in Vigny's case. But these are private matters and thus cannot and should not be publicized in verses for all to read; they belong to one's intimate life and are not suitable material for the generality of literature, since neither the absence of sexual relations nor unsatisfactory sexual relations represent a typical or widespread human experience.

Even so, had these poets sung directly of their baser troubles (for they are indeed base, however they may be used poetically), had they bared their souls in all their nakedness rather than in padded bathing suits, then the sheer violence of their sorrow's root cause might have yielded some admirable lamentations. This would to a certain extent have eliminated — by bringing everything out in the open — the social ridicule that, rightly or wrongly, attaches to these emotional banalities. If a man is a coward, he can either not talk about it (and this is the wiser course), or he can say point-blank, "I'm a coward." In the one case he has the advantage of dignity, in the other the advantage of sincerity; either way he escapes being comical, since in the first case he has said nothing and so there's nothing to laugh at, while in the second case there's nothing to discover, for he himself revealed his cowardice. But the coward who feels the need to prove he isn't one, or to affirm that cowardice is universal, or to confess his weakness in a vague, metaphorical way that reveals nothing but also hides nothing

— this man is ridiculous to the general public and irritating to the intelligence. This is the kind of man I see in the pessimistic poets and in all those who raise their private sorrows to the status of universal ones.

How can I take Leopardi's atheism seriously or react to it sympathetically, if I know it could have been cured by sexual intercourse? How can I sincerely respect and respond to Antero de Quental's wistfulness, sadness and despair, if I realize that it all sprang directly from his forlorn heart, which never found its complement — physical or psychological, it matters little — in the real world? How can I be impressed by Vigny's pessimism apropos women, by his exemplary and outrageous "*La Colère de Samson*,"[21] if in the very outrage of the poem I recognize the "loved by few or loved poorly, and suffering cruelly on that account" of the critic Faguet,[22] if I see it's but the lofty expression of a cuckold's ordinary torment?

How can anyone take seriously the argument "I'm shy with women, therefore God doesn't exist," which is at the heart of Leopardi's work? How not reject Antero de Quental's conclusion that "I'm sorry I don't have a woman who loves me, therefore sorrow is a universal condition"? How can I accept, and not instinctively disdain, Vigny's attitude: "I'm not loved in the way I'd like, therefore women are vile, mean and despicable creatures, with none of the goodness and nobility of men"? Absolute principles, and therefore false; ridiculous and therefore unaesthetic. Rarely does a work with perfect dignity and self-assurance provoke public laughter, for either it will have a quality that captivates the masses, even if they don't understand it, or it will have a quality that's beyond them, and so they won't laugh for the simple reason that they don't see. The common people don't laugh at *The Critique of Pure Reason*.[23]

The mind's dignity is to acknowledge that it is limited and that reality[24] is outside it. To acknowledge, with or without dismay, that nature's laws do not bend to our wishes, that the world exists independently of our will, that our own sadness proves nothing about the moral condition of the stars or even of the people who pass by our windows — in this acknowledgment lies the mind's true purpose and the soul's rational dignity.

Even now, when nothing attracts me but death (which is "nothing"), I quickly lean out the window to see the cheerful groups of farm workers going home, singing almost religiously, in the still evening air. I recognize that their life is happy. I recognize it at the edge of the grave that I myself will dig, and I recognize it with the ultimate pride of not failing to recognize it. What does the personal sorrow that torments me have to do with the universal greenness of the trees, with the natural cheer of these young men and women? What does the wintry end into which I am sinking have to do with the spring that's now in the world thanks to natural laws, whose action on the course of the stars makes the roses bloom, and whose action in me makes me end my life?

How I would diminish before my own eyes and, in truth, before everything and everyone, were I to say right now that the spring is sad, that the flowers suffer, that the rivers lament, that there's anguish and anxiety in the farm workers' song, and all because Álvaro Coelho de Athayde, the fourteenth[25] Baron of Teive, realized with regret that he can't write the books he wanted to!

I confine to myself the tragedy that's mine. I suffer it, but I suffer it face to face, without metaphysics or sociology. I admit that I'm conquered by life, but not humbled by it.[26]

Many people have tragedies, and if we count the incidental ones, then all people do. But it's up to everyone who's a man not to speak of his tragedy, and it's up to everyone who's an artist either to be a man and keep his trouble to himself, writing or singing about other things, or to extract from it — with lofty determination — a universal lesson.

✳

I feel I have attained the full use of my reason. And that's why I'm going to[27] kill myself.

✳

Forced as a slave to be a gladiator, were I to brandish the sword it would be my defeat; by rejecting it, it will be my freedom. And I solemnly salute Fate with my penultimate gesture, before the final one whereby, admitting that I'm conquered, I'll make myself a conqueror.

In the arena where Caesar has thrown us to fight in mortal combat, the man who dies is the conquered, and the one who kills is the conqueror.

✳

A gladiator whose fate as a slave condemned him to the arena, I take my bow, without fearing the Caesar who's in this circus surrounded by stars. I bow low, without pride, since a slave has nothing to be proud of, and without joy, since a man condemned to die can hardly smile. I bow so as not to fail the law, which so completely failed me. But having taken my bow, I drive into my chest the sword that won't serve me in combat.

If the conquered man is the one who dies and the conqueror the one who kills, then by this act, admitting that I'm conquered, I make myself a conqueror.

Appendix

The Duel

We believe that duels should be categorically outlawed, not because they're dangerous and put lives at risk, but because they're too ludicrous a phenomenon to deserve the right to exist.

The duel! The modern duel!

In centuries past, when the duel had a place, when it fit into the psychology of the day, then okay, maybe I can see it. But today? It's out of keeping with current social mores, except insofar as it's plain stupid.

And there's another point to consider. Duels, besides being stupid as proofs of honor, are usually fought by people who have no honor to prove. Masked bandits, pimps and [......], if they're at all courageous, which still happens often enough, are quick to avenge on the field of honor the slightest affront to the honor they don't have.

The psychology of these people is beyond our grasp, but we've seen enough to conclude that stupidity is what predominates.

Three Pessimists[28]

[written by Pessoa in English]

THE THREE ARE VICTIMS OF THE ROMANTIC illusion, and they are especially victims because none of them had the romantic temperament. All three were destined to be classicists, and, in their manner of writing, Leopardi always was, Vigny[29] almost always, Quental[30] only so in the perfect cast of his sonnets. The sonnet is nonclassical, however, though, owing to its epigrammatic basis, it should be so.

All three were thinkers — Quental most of all, for he had real metaphysical ability, Leopardi afterwards, Vigny last, but still far ahead in that respect of the other French romantics, with whom, naturally, he should be compared in that respect.

The romantic illusion consists in taking literally the Greek philosopher's phrase that man is the measure of all things, or sentimentally the basic affirmation of critical philosophy, that all the world is a concept of ours. These affirmations, harmless to the mind in themselves, are particularly dangerous, and often absurd, when they become dispositions of temperament and not merely concepts of the mind.

The romantic refers everything to himself and is incapable of thinking objectively. What happens to him happens to the universality of things. If he is sad, the world not only seems, but is, wrong.

Suppose a romantic falls in love with a girl of a higher social station, and that this difference in class prevents their marriage, or, perhaps, even love on her side, for social conventions go deep into the soul, as reformers often ignore. The romantic will say, "I cannot have the girl I love because of social conventions; therefore social conventions are bad." The realist, or classicist, would have said, "Fate has been unkind to me in making me fall in love with a girl I cannot have," or "I have been imprudent in cultivating an impossible love." His love would not be less; his reason would be more. It would never occur to a realist to attack social conventions on the score that they produce such results for him, or individual troubles of any kind. He knows that laws are good or bad generally, that no law can fit every particular case come under it, that the best law will produce terrible injustices in particular cases. But he does not conclude that there should be no law; he concludes only that the people involved in those particular cases have been unlucky.

*

To make realities of our particular feelings and dispositions, to convert our moods into measures of the universe, to believe that, because we want justice or love justice, Nature must necessarily have the same want or the same love, to suppose that because a thing is bad it can be made better without making it worse — these are romantic attitudes, and they define all minds which are incapable of conceiving reality as something outside themselves, infants crying for sublunary moons.

Almost all modern social reform is a romantic concept, an effort to invest reality with our wishes. The degrading concept of the perfectibility of man [......]

The very pagan concept of the origin of evil proclaims the pagan tendency to be conscious of objective reality. The pagan conceives this world as governed directly by gods, which are men on a larger scale, but, like men, good and evil, or good and evil in turns, who have caprices like men and moods as men have, and [who are] governed ultimately by an abstract compelling Fate, under which both gods and men move in logical orbits, but according to a reason which transcends ours, if it does not oppose it. This may be no more than a dream, like all theories, but it does conform to the course and appearance of the world; it does make the existence of evil and injustice an explainable thing. The gods do to us what we do to animals and lesser things.

Compare with this the Christian thesis that the evil in the world is the product of a benevolent and omnipotent God, and the higher logic of the pagan theory will at once be seen. The existence of many gods may or may not satisfy the mind; the existence of erring and sinning gods may or may not satisfy the mind; but the existence of many and erring gods does satisfy the mind in respect of the existence of caprice, evil and injustice in the course of this apparent world.

LEOPARDI[31]

[written by Pessoa in English]

THIS IS ONE OF THE CASES IN WHICH WE MUST ALL be Freuds. It is impossible to lean not to sexual explanation, because the social behaviors Leopardi erects of his own problem [......]

The worst of this sort of tragedy is that it is comic. It is not comic in the sense that Swinburne's love poems are comic.

"I am shy with women: therefore there is no God" is highly unconvincing metaphysics.

In the Garden of Epictetus

"THE PLEASANT SIGHT OF THESE FRUITS AND THE coolness given off by these leafy trees are yet other solicitations of Nature," said the Master, "encouraging us to abandon ourselves to the higher delights of a serene mind. There is no better hour for our admittedly useless meditation on life than now, when the sun has not yet set but the day's heat has subsided, and a breeze seems to lift from off the cooling fields.

"Many are the questions that occupy our thoughts, and great is the time we waste to discover that we cannot resolve them. To lay them aside, as one who passes by without wanting to see, is too much to expect from a man and too little from a god. To devote ourselves to them as to a lord would be to sell what we don't have.

"Sit still with me in the shade of these green trees, which have no weightier thought than the withering of their leaves when autumn arrives, or the stretching of their many stiff fingers into the cold sky of the passing winter. Sit still with me and meditate on how useless effort is, how alien the will, and on how our very meditation is no more useful than effort, and no more our own than the will. Meditate, too, on how a life that wants nothing can have no weight in the flux of things, but a life that wants everything can likewise have no weight in the flux of things, since it cannot obtain everything, and to obtain less than everything is not worthy of souls that seek the truth.

"A tree's shade is worth more than the knowledge of truth, my sons, for a tree's shade is true while it lasts, and the knowledge of truth is false in its very truth. The leaves' greenness is worth more, for a right understanding, than a great thought, for the leaves' greenness is something you can show others, but you can never show them a great thought We are born without knowing how to talk, and we die without having known how to express ourselves. Our life runs its course between the silence of one who cannot speak and the silence of one who wasn't understood, and around it hovers — like a bee where there are no flowers — a useless, inscrutable destiny."

The Man from Porlock

THE MARGINAL NOTES TO THE HISTORY OF LITERATURE record, as a curiosity, the manner in which Coleridge composed and wrote his "Kubla Khan." This quasi-poem is one of the most extraordinary poems of English literature, the greatest of all literatures after Greek. And its extraordinary fabric is intimately linked to its extraordinary genesis.

The poem — Coleridge tells us — was composed in a dream. He was living at the time in an isolated farmhouse, between the villages of Porlock and Linton. One day, after taking a pain reliever, he fell asleep for three hours, during which (he says) he composed the poem, whose images and corresponding verbal expressions arose in his spirit together and without effort. Once awake, he proceeded to write down what he had composed. He had already written thirty lines when a visitor — "a man from Porlock" — was announced. Coleridge felt obliged to receive the visitor, who detained him for about an hour. When he went back to transcribing what he'd composed in his dream, he realized that he had forgotten the rest of what he had to write. All he could remember was the poem's conclusion — twenty-four more lines.

And so we have this fragment or these fragments known as "Kubla Khan" — the beginning and end of something wondrously otherworldly, couched in mysterious terms that our imagination cannot humanly picture, and we shudder before our ignorance of what the plot might have been. Edgar Allan Poe (Coleridge's disciple, whether he knew it or not) never, in verse or prose, touched the Other World in such a spontaneous way or with such frightful plenitude. In Poe's writings, with all of their coldness, something of our world remains, albeit negatively; in "Kubla Khan" everything is foreign, from the Beyond, and this no-one-knows-quite-what takes place in an Orient that's impossible but that the poet positively saw.

*

Coleridge gives us no details about that "man from Porlock" whom so many, like me, have cursed. Was it by sheer coincidence that this unknown interrupter showed up and obstructed a communication between the abyss and life? Or was the apparent coincidence born of one of those real, occult presences that seem to deliberately thwart even the intuitive, lawful revelation of the Mysteries, as well as the transcription of dreams in which some such revelation might lurk?

Whatever the case, I believe that Coleridge's experience is an extreme example, serving as a vivid allegory of what happens to all of us when in this world we try, with the sensibility that goes into art, to communicate — like false pontiffs — with the Other World of ourselves.

All of us compose our works in a dream, even if we compose them while awake. And "the man from Porlock," the inevitable interrupter, inwardly visits all of us, even if we never have visitors. All that we truly think or feel, all that we truly are — as soon as we try to express it, even if only to ourselves — suffers the fatal interruption of that visitor who we also are, that person from the outside who is inside us all, more real in life than we ourselves, than the living summation of all we've learned, all we think we are, and all we'd like to be.

We all, because we're weak, must receive that visitor, that interrupter — forever unknown since he's not "someone," although he's us; forever anonymous since he's "impersonal," although alive — between the beginning and the end of a poem, composed in its entirety but not allowed by us to be written. And all that really survives, whether we be great or small artists, are fragments of we don't know what but which would have been, if realized, the very expression of our soul.

If only we knew how to be children, such that we wouldn't have visitors, nor feel obliged to receive them if we did! But we don't want to keep that nonexistent visitor waiting; we don't want to offend that "stranger," *who is us*. And so, instead of what could have been, we're left with merely what is: instead of the poem, or the *opera omnia*, just the beginning and the end of something lost — *disjecta membra* which, as Carlyle said, are what remain of any poet, or of any man.

The Impersonation of a Stoic

Antonio Tabucchi

The hazily sketched figure called the Baron of Teive issues from one of the commonest literary stereotypes: the manuscript discovered by chance. Not in Zaragoza, like the manuscript of Potocki;* nor in bizarre circumstances, like that of Poe's Arthur Gordon Pym; nor in eighteenth-century boudoirs and convents (obviously French and a bit perverse) of diabolical lovers and impassioned nuns. The manuscript of the Baron of Teive was found lying in the drawer of a hotel room, where it had been placed to keep it safe from one or another "hotel worker's not very clean hands."

This fleeting figure plays out his role quickly in the "subjective tragedy" of the stageless theater that is Pessoa's literary oeuvre. A dramatic character — such is the baron's status and as such he should be read. Read perhaps as the Platonic idea of a character who needs no biography to exist. As for the autobiographical

---

* In his lifetime the Polish count Jan Potocki (1761-1815) published excerpts from his curious novel titled *The Manuscript Found in Zaragoza*, supposedly the transcription of a travel narrative found by an official from Napoleon's army in Spain, but the complete text did not see print until 1989. The count, perhaps it is worth mentioning, is reported to have blown his brains out with a bullet he himself smelted from silver. [–Ed.]

component that Pessoa might have conferred on him, I'm afraid it's too late for us to believe in this. Like Tolstoy and Balzac, Pessoa thought of being many things, but unlike the great nineteenth-century novelists, he knew that there are so many who think of being the same thing that they can't all be it. If those ingenious novelists conquered the world before the twentieth century woke them up out of their beds, Pessoa painfully and unforgettably woke up in his century and saw that the world was alien and that it included the whole earth plus the solar system, the Milky Way and the Indefinite.* It is this consciousness of our human condition, at both the general and acutely personal levels, that makes him the greatest novelist without a novel and the most inexorably modern writer — a point of arrival from which we must in some way or another depart again.

If he himself made it impossible for us to believe that there's any trace of real life in the pseudo lives he created, it's only natural for us to wonder if there was any reality in the life he actually lived, in that "provisional, visible representation of himself," as he wrote on a photo sent to his Aunt Anica. So is everything false? Including this utterly conventional Baron of Teive, who's not a true stoic but the cliché of a stoic, the cliché of an embittered man, the cliché of a suicide? On the contrary: nothing could be truer. He's made of the truth alluded to by Pushkin when he said, "I've shed countless tears

---

* This and the previous sentence contain almost direct citations from Álvaro de Campos's "The Tobacco Shop." [—ED.]

58

over fiction." The real stoic isn't the Baron of Teive but the poet who imagined him, and perhaps we too are stoics — we, the inhabitants of this moribund millennium, who've been taught that we didn't after all dream of a butterfly but that the butterfly perhaps dreamed us; we who can no longer be the lizard that had its tail cut off and that waits, in accord with nature's laws, for the tail to grow back but who must, instead, be the lizardless tail that twitchingly waits, in accord with no law, for the lizard to grow back.*

July 1999

---

* Alludes to two lines from "The Tobacco Shop": "Perhaps you've merely existed, as when a lizard has its tail cut off / And the tail keeps on twitching, without the lizard." [–Ed.]

POSTMORTEM

RICHARD ZENITH

I transferred to Teive my speculations on certainty, which lunatics have in greater abundance than anyone.

— Fernando Pessoa*

If men knew how to meditate on the mystery of life, if they knew how to feel the thousand complexities which spy on the soul in every single detail of action, then they would never act — they wouldn't even live. They would kill themselves from fright, like those who commit suicide to avoid being guillotined the next day.

— Bernardo Soares**

The Baron of Teive took fright. Or rather: a frightened Pessoa created the baron to save his own skin. He transferred all of his implacable lucidity to the poor nobleman, who couldn't bear it, because the lucidity was too much and because his role didn't call for him to bear it. The Baron of Teive was born to die.

---

* From a fragmentary note recorded in the black notebook containing Teive's earliest writings.

** From Text 188 of my own translation of *The Book of Disquiet* (London: Penguin Books, 2001), which is based on the Portuguese edition I edited in 1998. Other English-language versions of this work, including the Exact Change volume translated by Alfred Mac Adam, are based on earlier Portuguese editions, and consequently the text numbers cited here will not correspond.

All of Pessoa's dozens of alter egos, whom he called "heteronyms," were instruments of exorcism and redemption. They were born to save him from this life that he felt ill-equipped to live, or that offended his aesthetic and moral sensibilities, or that simply bored him. But the Baron of Teive took on his creator's most dangerous quality: unbridled reason. "My mind has always ruled my feelings," confesses the baron, and when he arrives at the conclusion that it "is impossible to live life according to reason," his mind imposes suicide as the rational way out. Or Pessoa, forever faithful to literature, imposed it.

If Bernardo Soares, the alter ego entrusted with *The Book of Disquiet*, was classified not as a heteronym but as a semiheteronym, since his personality (Pessoa wrote in 1935) "doesn't differ from my own but is a mere mutilation of it,"* then the same label may be applied to the Baron of Teive, who was even mutilated in his flesh. The painful experience of having his left leg amputated was an important lesson in the education of the stoical nobleman, who endured the surgery without general anesthesia, but it no doubt had a symbolic function as well. "Everything is symbols" (from an Álvaro de Campos poem) may not be a valid principle in the world we live in, but it aptly characterizes the universe according to Pessoa.

Pessoa compared his two "mutilations" in a prose passage written for his preface to a planned collection of

---

* From a letter to Adolfo Casais Monteiro dated 13 January 1935, included in *The Selected Prose of Fernando Pessoa* (New York: Grove Press, 2001), p. 251.

his heteronymic works:

The assistant bookkeeper Bernardo Soares and the Baron of Teive —
both are me-ishly extraneous characters — write with the same basic
style, the same grammar, and the same careful diction. In other words,
they both write with the style that, good or bad, is my own. I compare
them because they are two instances of the very same phenomenon —
an inability to adapt to real life — motivated by the very same causes.
But although the Portuguese is the same in the Baron of Teive and in
Bernardo Soares, their styles differ. That of the aristocrat is intellectual,
without images, a bit — how shall I put it? — stiff and constrained,
while that of his middle-class counterpart is fluid, participating in music
and painting but not very architectural. The nobleman thinks clearly,
writes clearly, and controls his emotions, though not his feelings; the
bookkeeper controls neither emotions nor feelings, and what he thinks
depends on what he feels.

It was the baron's inability to control his immediate
feelings — and even, at the end of the day, his emotions — that prompted him to call it quits. "Powerful as
thought is," he observed in his only dated text (p. 21), "it
can do nothing to quell rebellious emotions." He could
tolerate and even sneer at pain, but he couldn't tolerate the humiliation of being subject to the whims of
others, and for him, as in the rest of Pessoa, the inner
self that felt and dreamed was an outsider, someone else,
another. What killed the baron wasn't just the ruthless
logic of his ultrarational mind but its limitations and
his refusal to accept them — pride, in other words. Of all
the writer-actors that performed in Pessoa's theater of

himself, Teive was the one who most completely embodied lucidity and pride, qualities that were fatally linked in the play's producer.

Bernardo Soares was no more able than Teive to adapt to the practical side of life, but he didn't despair for that reason. True to his middle-class upbringing, he tried to get what he could out of the humdrum life he was given. And so he reports, at the beginning of a passage from *The Book of Disquiet* (Text 444): "Everything has become unbearable except for life," which in its ensemble of banal events — such as a ray of sunlight entering his office, or a vendor's chant rising up to the window of his rented room — still "brings relief" to the assistant bookkeeper. He takes great pleasure in observing and narrating, with wistful fondness or even discreet enthusiasm, the little things that fill up and surround his daily life. He records the changes of seasons and weather, describes Lisbon's squares, streetcars and building façades, tells about the barber, the delivery boys, the grocer bent over a sack of potatoes, the woman who sells bananas on the Rua da Prata. But the baron, dry and linear, a bit "stiff," as Pessoa put it, doesn't really know how to enjoy simple things. He speaks at one point of the "small emotions" of life in the country that remained after he'd renounced his ambition to be a serious writer, but they couldn't distract him from his existential anguish.

The baron stoically endures his suffering, but with no transcendence, just the boastful rhetoric ("whining is for women" he writes) of an emotionally tough but profoundly frustrated male, who seems to have suffered from impotence. Bernardo Soares, more Epicurean than stoical (he cultivates a "refined Epicureanism" according to the opening passage of his *Book*)* not only endures suffering, he explores and exploits it. In fact he fuses, for his personal use, the two Greek philosophies: "Since stoicism is after all just a stringent form of Epicureanism, I try to get some amusement out of my misfortune" (Text 398). Teive notes, with unadulterated bitterness, that his entire life "has been a battle lost on the map"; Soares makes the exact same observation but — aware that he's going to lose — takes pleasure in mapping out the details of his retreats (Text 193).

Soares's "Sentimental Education" (written in the 1910s and attributed to him only later) contrasts sharply with *The Education of the Stoic*. Soares's essay, included in *The Book of Disquiet*, teaches that a good dreamer should avoid suffering, but not "like the Stoics or the early Epicureans." He should, instead, "seek pleasure in pain," for which there are three methods: 1) to hyperanalyze pain until this practice absorbs everything, such that "there will be nothing left of pain but an indefinite substance for analysis"; 2) to create "another I, charged with suffering — in and for us — everything we suffer"; and 3) to "concentrate intensely on our anxieties and sufferings," feeling them to such an excessive degree that they "bring the pleasure of excess."

---

* Although marked by Pessoa as the "beginning passage," some editions place this passage elsewhere.

The Education of the Stoic, despite its title that seems to promise theoretical instruction and/or practical advice, is a strictly personal narrative, a kind of "true life story" made up of negative lessons that recall Bernardo Soares, Ricardo Reis, the later Álvaro de Campos, and Pessoa himself. Although these and Pessoa's other self-manifestations were carefully individuated from one another in tone, style, outlook and concerns, there was a certain promiscuity between the nobleman and the bookkeeper (as there was, to a lesser degree, between Soares and Campos as a prose writer). When Teive writes "I belong to a generation... that lost its faith in the gods of the old religions as well as in the gods of modern nonreligions," he borrows a formula employed on various occasions by Bernardo Soares (at the beginning of Text 306, for instance). Or did Soares filch it from his aristocratic colleague? In fact the formula goes back to one of Pessoa's autobiographical notes dating from the 1910s, but both Soares and Teive shared this and other quite specific expressions beginning in 1928, the year Teive was "born" on paper and Soares probably assumed authorship of *The Book of Disquiet*. (*The Book* was initially attributed to another heteronymic bookkeeper, Vicente Guedes. Soares, before replacing Guedes, was a writer of short stories.)

The manuscript evidence indicates that the baron's earliest writings are twenty-nine pages of fragmentary prose passages contained in a small black notebook. These seem to have been produced in the space of several weeks or months, and though none of them is dated, the date contained in the "news report" of the suicide (p. 7) was initially 12 July 1928, Pessoa having subsequently changed the 8 to 0. The Teive pages are immediately preceded by a poem dated 6 August 1928.

It was in the passages from this notebook that Pessoa sketched out the baron's biography: a solitary childhood, suggesting that he was an only son; university studies leading to a degree; a close relationship with his mother, who died when the baron was already full-grown; a well-to-do life spent on an estate not far from Lisbon; travel abroad, at least to Paris, where he frequented the French nobility; difficulty entering into sexual relations with women; and the amputation of his left leg not long before his suicide, which occurred on 11 July 1920 (the report of the tragedy in the *Diário de Notícias* having been published the following day). It was also in the black notebook that Pessoa roughed out, or tried to rough out, *The Only Manuscript of the Baron of Teive*, when he still didn't know if that was the name (placed in doubt by a graphic sign) he wanted to give the new heteronym. Among the eighteen passages of Teive's work found on loose sheets, one carries a date, 27 March 1930, while another registers the aristocrat's full name: Álvaro Coelho de Athayde, fourteenth Baron of Teive. The same name appears in the notebook, but designated as the twentieth rather than fourteenth Baron of Teive.

If the character of the baron almost certainly took shape in the summer of 1928, the dramatic finale of his existence seems to have been at least partly conceived a decade and a half earlier. Among the various notebooks, thousands of loose sheets and assorted paper scraps that make up Pessoa's archives there's an envelope, postmarked in 1912, on which the author scribbled: "Ms. found in the drawer of a hotel room." These are precisely the circumstances in which Pessoa discovered Teive's last and only surviving manuscript, according to the account from a loose sheet (the same one that contains the title *Education of the Stoic*) transcribed at the front of this volume (p. 1). And Teive's "womb," the black notebook, contains the isolated memo "Manuscript found in a drawer," followed by this intriguing phrase in parentheses: "The seduction of Maria Adelaide." Could it be that the baron — according to the fiction that Pessoa never fully fleshed out — finished writing (or, rather, left unfinished) his *Education of the Stoic* in a hotel room, where he'd finally managed to seduce a girl named Maria, before heading back to his estate in Macieira to commit suicide? Might he at least have had that satisfaction before his tragic end?

The baron's obsession with his sexual problem is alluded to in a memorandum on the very first of the black notebook's twenty-nine pages dedicated to Teive: "Second chapter. Why the Baron didn't seduce more girls." It was a problem frequently referred to in Pessoa's personal notes from the preceding years and especially in his automatic writings, with Henry More — the most loquacious of his astral correspondents — having repeatedly promised that a pretty girl would soon enter his life to cure him of his virginity.*

Naturally enough, all of the heteronyms — whose "otherness" couldn't escape the bounds of their creator's psychology — were resolute bachelors whose infrequent relationships with women were generally abstract, internalized. Lydia and the other girlfriends of Ricardo Reis are bodiless, speechless interlocutors; we don't even know the name of Alberto Caeiro's only love; and the bisexual naval engineer whose motto is "to feel everything in every way" feels his lovers most intensely when they're far away — in another country or in his distant past. And the heteronyms don't usually complain about the paucity of their amorous conquests. If they're alone, it's because they're better off that way.

Love, as concept or theory, always had a place in Pessoa's literary work, but it was only in 1928, by way of the Baron of Teive, that it took on flesh, so to speak, and became a problem — a sexual problem — begging to be resolved. And why only at that late date, the year Pessoa turned forty? The answer to that question will help us understand the raison d'être of this heteronym — Pessoa's thinnest disguise.

The late 1920s marked a new phase in Pessoa's life. He had abandoned not only the vanguard movements promulgated by him in the 1910s — Futurism, Sensationism

---

* Pessoa's main astral correspondent was not a pure fiction but the "spirit" of the poet and philosopher Henry More (1614-87), one of the so-called Cambridge Platonists. A group of Pessoa's automatic writings can be found in *The Selected Prose of Fernando Pessoa*, pp. 103ff.

and Intersectionism, these last two being his own brain-children — but also his long-standing interest in founding literary magazines and publishing houses (several of which he did found and run, though never with great success). Sensing, perhaps, that his years were already fatally numbered, he began to write about himself with unprecedented transparency (even as the baron, on the eve of his death, acquires "an emotional clarity in my soul and a mental clarity in my intellect that give me the force of words"); he turned his irony into an instrument for revealing, rather than concealing, his inner self; and at the same time that he endeavored to consolidate his oeuvre he "let himself go," literarily speaking, to arrive more directly at whom he thought he might be.

In 1932 Pessoa, writing about the heteronyms to João Gaspar Simões, his future biographer, announced that "it's too late, and hence absurd, to pretend they're completely independent,"* but this pretended independence had started to crumble long before that, not only in the way Pessoa planned to publish his/their works but in the very way he, in their names, wrote. "The poet is a faker," asserted Pessoa in his signature poem, "Autopsychography," but the faking came to be a mere formal device (the use of heteronyms), while the poet became increasingly open, naked, himself even when he

* The cited letter to João Gaspar Simões was dated 28 July 1932 (*The Selected Prose of Fernando Pessoa*, p. 247). In a previous letter to Gaspar Simões, dated 18 November 1930, Pessoa explained that he had sublimated his sexual instinct in two self-published poems written in English: the homosexual "Antinöus" (1918) and the heterosexual "Epithalamium" (1921).

was "another." It was almost hand in hand that the Baron of Teive, the disquieted Bernardo Soares, and Álvaro de Campos of "The Tobacco Shop" (written in January of 1928) entered onto the stage of Pessoa's dramatized life, giving rise to the most poignant, self-analytical period of his oeuvre. It was the moment of semiheteronymy, for Campos in his new, introspective mode had ceased being a true "other." The masks — at least these three — had become almost indistinguishable from the man who had fashioned them.

Pessoa, who rekindled his only amorous liaison in 1929, only to let it snuff out definitively a few months later, used his three almost-me-anothers to express, and to try to discover, what he felt in this underexplored department of his life. While Campos nostalgically recalls the various women, and in particular an English blonde, with whom he could have hooked up, the assistant book-keeper — who was loved only once, didn't return the love he was shown, and considered the experience to be "a weariness beyond all tedium" (*Book of Disquiet*, Text 235) — justifies his chaste preference through various rationales. He argues at one point that "the repression of love sheds much more light on its nature than does the actual experience of it" (Text 271), and at another that love is a mere illusion, since, when we love someone else, "it's our own concept — our own selves — that we love" (Text 112). But there's also a passage (Text 113) in which his theory that it's better to observe than to experience love is called "a complicated jabber to fill the ears of my intelligence, to make it almost forget that at heart I'm just timid, with no aptitude for life."

Although the baron at a certain point blames his social position for having ruined his "chance to marry a simple girl who could perhaps have made me happy" (like the narrator of "The Tobacco Shop," had he married the daughter of his washwoman?), it's clear that the baron's larger problem with the opposite sex was more immediate, more carnal. The servant girls of his estate, all of them available and possibly even eager to be seduced, were either too big or too small for their boss, or too vivacious, too plain-looking, or too something else. In the person of the "automatically shy" baron, Pessoa made his frankest confession of his own sexual awkwardness and inexperience.

No less frustrating for the Baron of Teive was his inability to produce finished literary works, or — in the more grandiose words of the *Education*'s second subtitle — "the impossibility of producing superior art." This frustration wasn't, in fact, so different from the sexual one, as can be deduced from the baron's longest prose fragment ("To think that I considered...," p. 34). After several paragraphs in which the failed author complains of his inadequate willpower to produce an oeuvre commensurate with his intellectual capacity, he proceeds to criticize the "three great pessimistic poets" — Giacomo Leopardi, Alfred de Vigny and Antero de Quental — for making "universal tragedies out of the sad comedies of their private woes," which are none other than their sexual disappointments. In the final paragraphs he returns to his own tragedy, that of failing to write the books he wanted to, saying that he prefers — with greater nobility than Leopardi and company — to suffer in private, "without metaphysics or sociology." We need not bring in Freud to conclude that Pessoa sublimated his sexual instincts in his literary work, for he himself says as much. When that work didn't turn out the way he wanted, he felt a frustration analogous to that of men (or of women, though Pessoa, when it came to the opposite sex, wasn't any less chauvinistic than other males of his generation) who don't succeed in their attempted sexual conquests.

The anxiety rising out of the gap between his projected works and those he actually achieved on paper was always present in Pessoa, but it increased with age. He felt, on the one hand, that he'd lost the intensity and stamina of his youth, as intimated by a late Campos poem: "How long it's been since I could write / A long poem!" (dated 9 August 1934). On the other hand, twenty years of literary incontinence had left Pessoa floundering in a sea of written scraps and fragments: pages upon pages of an unassembled *Faust*, over five hundred passages of a *Book of Disquiet* whose title perfectly defined its organizational state, hundreds of finished and unfinished poems, isolated scenes from projected plays and short stories, scattered pieces of essays on scores of topics, and dozens of more or less elaborate plans — likewise incomplete, indefinite, contradictory — for how to publish his massive but piecemeal output.

Looking at the literary output of others, made up of "lengthy and finished works," Bernardo Soares confesses that he feels terrible envy (Text 85). He repeatedly complains (Texts 152, 169 and 231), just like the baron, of the incomplete and imperfect state of his writings, and he likewise claims that he wouldn't be especially upset if tomorrow they all went up in smoke (Text 118). Unlike Teive, Soares is unable to give up this "drug" — writing — that he keeps on taking, even though he abhors it (Text 152). But the dreamy assistant bookkeeper, always shrewder and more pragmatic than we expect, notes in yet another passage (Text 64): "I weep over my imperfect pages, but if future generations read them, they will be more touched by my weeping than by any perfection I might have achieved, since perfection would have kept me from weeping and, therefore, from writing. Perfection never materializes." The baron, quite to the contrary, won't admit weeping, won't admit imperfection, and is devoid of self-irony. Proud to the core, his nobility turns out to be his greatest limitation. Soares, who's nobody in this world, "can dream he is the Roman emperor, but the King of England cannot, for in his dreams the King of England is precluded from being any king other than the one he is" (Text 171). Teive, condemned by his blood to be a "somebody," instinctively distrusts dreams, since, "a dream, when too lifelike or familiar, becomes a new reality, equally tyrannical." And in a passage from the black notebook he states, without ambiguity, "I rejected dreaming as a madman's or schoolgirl's vice."

Although he writes about the same themes (*The Book of Disquiet* also takes up the pessimists Leopardi, Vigny and Quental, in Text 278, and the theological problem of the existence of evil, in Texts 208 and 254), Bernardo Soares is diametrical in character to the Baron of Teive. He's a mirror image, an inverted likeness. Outwardly unaristocratic, the bookkeeper cultivates an interior aristocracy:

The aristocrat is the one who never forgets that he's never alone; that's why etiquette and decorum are the privilege of aristocracies. Let's internalize the aristocrat. Let's take him out of his gardens and drawing rooms and place him in our soul and in our consciousness of existing. Let's always treat ourselves with etiquette and decorum, with studied and for-other-people gestures. (Text 428)

Pessoa himself had definite aristocratic pretensions, based on rather dubious credentials: a few low-ranking noblemen among his father's ancestors. He left, among his papers, a detailed description of the Pessoa family arms which he had copied from an encyclopedia, along with the information (conjectural) that his surname is of noble, Germanic origin. His monarchic sympathies are most evident in his political writings (even if he grudgingly supported the Portuguese Republic), but his fascination with nobility crops up at frequent intervals throughout his work.

Pessoa was elitist, classist, and very politically in-correct, even for the norms of the period. His daily life, however, was not that much different from the one led, or endured, by the unmistakably humble Bernardo Soares. Humble, that is, in his outer circumstances. Which was lucky for him, since that meant he could only know and enjoy "*in the shade*, that nobility of spirit that makes no demands on life" (Text 45, my italics). The Baron of Teive, by contrast, had to bear the cross of his *public* aristocracy. He loathed the society that his aristocratic condition wouldn't let him avoid completely, but the worst thing was the generalized celebrity conferred on him by that same condition. Everyone knew, and perhaps laughed at the fact, that the baron was shy, that the baron never managed to take women to bed, that he'd been devastated by his mother's death, that he didn't care for duels or competitive games. Unwilling to impute, like the "three pessimists," his personal problems to higher causes, the proud baron opted for suicide.

If many of the heteronyms were vehicles that enabled Pessoa to flee his rather colorless existence and even, in a few cases, to do things he would have "really" liked to do himself, other personas emerged to justify that same existence, or they served in both capacities. The bucolic colors and calm informing the worlds of Alberto Caeiro and Ricardo Reis surely didn't reflect a strong desire in Pessoa to live in the countryside (though perhaps he would have liked to go to Brazil, where Ricardo Reis took refuge in 1919) but served him merely as necessary moments of serenity, a vicarious tranquillity. Far different was the case of Álvaro de Campos, for in a certain corner of his heart Pessoa dreamed of traveling abroad, of being in direct contact with Anglo-Saxon culture, of living with panache as a decadent dandy. But only in a certain corner of his heart. Nature imposes a fidelity to who we are, and Pessoa didn't have it in him to be an Álvaro de Campos, save on several occasions when he assumed that guise among literary pals and with Ophelia Queiroz, his one sweetheart.* And by the late 1920s Campos the dandy had gone into retirement. He had already, some years earlier, arrived at the conclusion that all the sensations experienced in his worldwide travels had been in vain, since "however much I felt I never felt enough,/ And life always pained me, it was always too little, and I was unhappy."** Disillusioned and worn out, the naval engineer returned to Lisbon, resigning himself to the quiet life of a spectator, equal to his inventor's life except in one particular: Pessoa had been spared all that strain and effort. He'd used Campos to enjoy, secondhand, a few wild adventures and also to prove that he, Pessoa, had been right not to waste his time and energy on real travel, since he would have ended up at the same

* Ophelia Queiroz reported to her great-niece that Pessoa showed up at several of their appointed rendezvous as Álvaro de Campos, and Gaspar Simões wrote that the same thing happened the first time he and a friend met, or thought they were going to meet, the poet Fernando Pessoa.
** From the poem "Time's Passage," in *Fernando Pessoa & Co.: Selected Poems* (New York: Grove Press, 1998), p. 154.

terminus as his world-weary heteronym: Lisbon and an incurable melancholy.

The Baron of Teive was a kindred experience. While Bernardo Soares retreated into his spiritualized, personal brand of aristocracy, the baron embodied the genealogical nobility Pessoa had always yearned for, at least in a certain corner of his heart. He created a baron made in his own image: a shy bachelor who spent his time thinking and writing. But the experiment flopped, as it had to, because with or without a mask and the *de rigeur* accouterments, Pessoa could never have kept the rules that govern a nobleman's life. The Baron of Teive, in his tragic failure as a titled aristocrat, was a validating proof that the kind of aristocracy practiced by Soares was the only one that suited Pessoa.

Teive also served in another capacity: as a warning, or reminder, that reason on its own is a blind alley. Endowed to excess with Pessoa's inexorable intelligence, the baron was missing the irony and spontaneity that functioned as redemptory counterweights in Soares and Campos. Teive "thinks clearly," thinks continuously, thinks relentlessly, and arrives at the clarity of sheer emptiness, but without the existential levity that allows the naval engineer to quip: "I'm beginning to know myself. I don't exist."* And the mordant bookkeeper, resorting to metaphor: "I'm the suburbs of a nonexistent town… the character of an unwritten novel" (Text 262). The unlucky

---

* The first line of an Álvaro de Campos poem, in *Fernando Pessoa & Co.*, p. 200.

baron lacked not only satisfying sexual experiences, finished literary works, his mother and his left leg; he lacked a sense of humor.

Even more than a warning, Teive — who died not because of his extreme lucidity but because of the pride it engendered — was a sacrificial victim. Pessoa needed Teive, or some heteronym like him, to die for his sins. And Pessoa's greatest sin was that — notwithstanding his unfailing habit of reducing everything to the final common denominator of nothing — he was human, with the normal attitudes and reactions that characterize the species. He couldn't escape the feelings of pride and vanity that his admirable intellectual powers naturally aroused, but he knew that those powers were also nothing, that they were no reason to take himself too seriously. He knew (as indicated in the first epigraph to this essay) that certainty is the province of lunatics, and that life, brief and absurd, should never be treated as a serious matter. And so he invented the baron, placed in him his own keen and proud intellect, and killed him with a smile that was anything but innocent.

NOTES

[1] *Manuscript found in a drawer:* Pessoa records his discovery on the same sheet containing the title and two subtitles of Teive's last and only surviving work (he having burned all his previous writings in the fireplace).

[2] *Bacon... thoughts of future generations:* In his last will, drafted in 1625, Francis Bacon wrote, "For my name and memory, I leave it to men's charitable speeches, and to foreign nations, and the next ages."

[3] *Diário de Notícias:* One of Portugal's major newspapers, then as now.

[4] *René:* The protagonist of François-René Chateaubriand's homonymous, largely autobiographical novel, published in 1802 as part of *Le Génie du christianisme.*

[5] *Vigny:* Alfred de Vigny (1797-1863), French author of poems, essays, plays and a novel. Disillusioned in love, unsuccessful in politics, and unenthusiastically received by the French Academy, he withdrew from society and became increasingly pessimistic in his writings, which recommended stoical resignation as the only noble response to the suffering that life condemns us to.

[6] *Antero de Quental:* A Portuguese poet and essayist (1842-91) remembered most of all for his sonnets, though his most ardent ambition was to be a philosopher. Politically engaged, he was a founder of Portugal's socialist movement. Quental's chronic pessimism, coupled with mental instability, worsened with age, until he finally committed suicide.

[7] *Leopardi was a philologist:* "Leopardi spoke Greek" (alternate version).

[8] *from a dying man:* This passage, typed on a loose sheet, is preceded by the words "*The Profession of Nonproducer* (title)." It was presumably a possible title for Teive's complete work rather than for just this passage.

[9] *Greek philosopher:* Protagoras.

[10] *Soame Jenyns's theory of evil*: A member of the English Parliament, Jenyns (1704-1787) was also a poet, critic and essayist. Pessoa refers here to an essay titled "A Free Enquiry into the Nature and Origin of Evil," which is also glossed in an Álvaro de Campos poem dated 18 December 1934.

[11] *Buridan's donkey*: The 14th-century French scholastic Jean Buridan, concerned with the problem of free will, is supposed to have asked what a donkey would do if, suffering equally from thirst and hunger, it stood at a point equidistant from a bucket of water and a bucket of hay.

[12] *that freezes the frightened man in his tracks*: "that makes the frightened man like a tree" (alternate version).

[13] *the world's armed men*: This passage, handwritten on a loose sheet, is the only one that carries a date, 27 March 1930.

[14] *I only agreed to a local anesthetic*: "I even refused a local anesthetic" / "But I would have accepted a local anesthetic, if such had been available at the time" (alternate versions).

[15] *(The seduction of Maria Adelaide)*: The story of Maria's seduction, like other narrative ideas recorded in the black notebook containing the baron's earliest writings, was never developed.

[16] *Why... seduce more girls*: This fragment, written on the first of the Teive pages in the black notebook, was preceded by the memo "Second Chapter."

[17] *neither the kiss of reality, nor the caress of the imaginary*: "neither the pleasure of reality, nor the pleasure of the imaginary" (alternate version).

[18] *Senancour, Amiel*: The works of French writer Étienne Pivert de Senancour (1770-1846) include the novel *Obermann* and are marked by a despondently melancholy tone. Henri-Frédéric Amiel (1821-81), a Swiss professor of aesthetics and philosophy, gained posthumous fame for his *Fragments d'un journal intime*, which influenced certain aspects of *The Book of Disquiet*.

[19] *from a love story*: This paragraph is followed, in the black notebook, by the following notes, which suggest that Pessoa planned to translate Teive's work into French and English:

> *Préface de l'auteur en tant que traducteur.*
> Preface of the author as translator. [in English in the original]
> No foreword of any kind should precede a work that is or that aspires to be a work of art. [in Portuguese in the original]

20 *Disjecta membra, said Carlyle*: Carlyle's exact words were: "*Disjecta membra* are all that we find of any Poet, or of any man" (in *On Heroes, Hero-Worship and the Heroic in History*).

21 *"La Colère de Samson"*: The poem is quoted in an Álvaro de Campos poem dated 9 July 1930.

22 *Faguet*: Émile Faguet (1847–1916) was one of the most prestigious French critics of his day.

23 *don't laugh at* The Critique of Pure Reason: "don't make fun of the Logician" (alternate version).

24 *reality*: "the universe" (alternate version).

25 *fourteenth*: Twentieth, according to the "news report" of Teive's suicide (p. 7).

26 *sociology. I admit... not humbled by it*: "sociology. Let me go to the grave with the name of Suicide, but not with the surname of [......]" (alternate version).

27 *why I'm going to*: "why I have to" (alternate version).

28 *Three Pessimists*: The title appears at the head of two distinct, typewritten fragments, separated here by an asterisk. Pessoa's English spelling has been Americanized, two changes were made in the punctuation, an erroneously employed definite article was dropped, and two words (placed in brackets) were added.

29 *Vigny*: See note 5.

30 *Quental*: See note 6.

Also available by Fernando Pessoa
from Exact Change:

The Book of Disquiet

Selected Exact Change Titles
FOR A COMPLETE CATALOGUE PLEASE VISIT
WWW.EXACTCHANGE.COM

Guillaume Apollinaire
THE POET ASSASSINATED

Louis Aragon
PARIS PEASANT

Antonin Artaud
WATCHFIENDS & RACK SCREAMS

Leonora Carrington
THE HEARING TRUMPET

Giorgio de Chirico
HEBDOMEROS

Salvador Dalí
OUI

Morton Feldman
GIVE MY REGARDS TO
EIGHTH STREET

Alfred Jarry
EXPLOITS & OPINIONS
OF DR. FAUSTROLL,
PATAPHYSICIAN

Franz Kafka
THE BLUE OCTAVO NOTEBOOKS

Lautréamont
MALDOROR

Gérard de Nerval
AURÉLIA

Pablo Picasso
THE BURIAL OF THE COUNT
OF ORGAZ

Raymond Roussel
HOW I WROTE CERTAIN
OF MY BOOKS

Kurt Schwitters
PPPPPP

Philippe Soupault
LAST NIGHTS OF PARIS

Gertrude Stein
EVERYBODY'S AUTOBIOGRAPHY

Stefan Themerson
BAYAMUS & CARDINAL
PÖLÄTÜO

Unica Zürn
DARK SPRING